Keri Hulme (1947–2021) was born in Christchurch, of Kāi Tahu, Kāti Māmoe and Orkney ancestry on her mother's side, and English on her father's. She identified Moeraki on the Otago East Coast as her tūrangawaewae-ngākau, and lived for over thirty years in a house she built herself, in Ōkārito on the West Coast.

Keri Hulme's novel the bone people, published by the Spiral Collective in 1984, was the most widely read and influential book of its time in Aotearoa New Zealand, and was published around the world in many languages, winning the Booker Prize in 1985. Her other books include poetry, The Silences Between (Moeraki Conversations) (1982), a novella, Lost Possessions (1985), and two collections of short stories, Te Kaihau | The Windeater (1986) and Stonefish (2004). She held the Robert Burns Fellowship at the University of Otago in 1977 and the Canterbury University Writing Fellowship in 1985, and was awarded the QEII Arts Council Scholarship in Letters in 1990.

The THW Classics collection
celebrates more than half a century of stellar publishing
at Te Herenga Waka—Victoria University of Wellington

The End of the Golden Weather by Bruce Mason 1962
Ngā Uruora by Geoff Park 1995
Breakwater by Kate Duignan 2001
Lifted by Bill Manhire 2005
Girls High by Barbara Anderson 1990
Portrait of the Artist's Wife by Barbara Anderson 1992
Wednesday to Come Trilogy by Renée 1985, 1986, 1991
In Fifteen Minutes You Can Say a Lot by Greville Texidor 1987
Eileen Duggan: Selected Poems edited by Peter Whiteford 1994
Denis Glover: Selected Poems edited by Bill Manhire 1995
The Vintner's Luck by Elizabeth Knox 1998
Man Alone by John Mulgan edited by Peter Whiteford 1935
Six by Six: Short Stories by New Zealand's Best Writers
edited by Bill Manhire 1989
Wild Dogs Under My Skirt by Tusiata Avia 2004
A.R.D. Fairburn: Selected Poems edited by Mac Jackson 1995
R.A.K. Mason: Collected Poems edited by Allen Curnow 1962
Ursula Bethell: Collected Poems edited by Vincent O'Sullivan 1985
Dick Seddon's Great Dive and other stories by Ian Wedde 1981
Lost Possessions by Keri Hulme 1985
Te Kaihau | The Windeater by Keri Hulme 1986

Lost Possessions

KERI HULME

TE HERENGA WAKA
UNIVERSITY PRESS

Te Herenga Waka University Press
Victoria University of Wellington
PO Box 600, Wellington
New Zealand
teherengawakapress.co.nz

First published 1985
This edition published 2022

A catalogue record for this book is available from
the National Library of New Zealand.

ISBN 9781776920198

Printed in Aotearoa New Zealand by Bluestar

They have left me.
The door is locked.
The room is entirely bare.
Quiet. Locked.
I have a towel. I wear it kiltwise.
There is a plastic rigger of water.
A small plastic bucket with a lid on it.
A thick little writing pad, of blank newsprint.
Do you remember buying them in Woolworths?
For threepence?
I'm writing with the felt-tip, orange barrel and black cap.
That is all.
My left eye is swelling.
My mouth has stopped bleeding where the teeth
cut into my lip.
I am feeling very strange as though, when they choked me, it did something to my brain.
Oxygen-starved cells therefore feeling high.
I ache.
I wait.
I think it is still Tuesday.

Let me get it down factually.
I was walking from my office in the main faculty building to the carpark.
I know it was just after six because I had glanced at my watch a moment before.
I was carrying my briefcase.
The evening was mild, windless.
I don't recall seeing anyone.
I was watching the swing of my briefcase, matching my pace.
Something I often do. A kind of meditative unwinding.
I don't know what was thrown round my neck—
it felt hard, rough. Maybe a thick leather belt.
I grasped at it with my right hand, then dropped my briefcase.
I was gagging. I blacked out.

They have not yet switched off the light.
I don't know whether it is day or night, or whether Wednesday has arrived. I do know that, left to itself, the human body settles into a 24 hour 40 minute cycle. I don't know how long it takes to settle into this cycle.
If I write one page, and relax and sleep until
I feel it is another day—

I think it is still Wednesday.
I had just used the bucket with the lid. I assume it is there for a lavatory.
I used a lot of the water to wash myself.
My fingers feel filthy although they appear clean.
The stench of the movement was still in the air when the door opened. There was the grate of a lock being turned, then a bolt being drawn.
A man with a brown paper bag over his head came just inside the room. He carried a long iron bar, a pry bar I believe it is called. He hefted it at me.
I stayed crouched on the floor.
I felt extremely silly, just a towel around my middle.
He sniffed, made an exclamation of disgust.
He dropped something on the floor.
'Is supper, man.'
It is an apple.

Thursday

My swollen eye has firmed; I feel the bruising must be turning from purple to yellow. My lip has scabbed over.
The numbness, giddyheadedness, has gone.
I feel fully aware, with a definite purpose.
My first instinct, to write notes, was a good one.
Keep a record. It may prove useful evidence. I can tuck them into my towel, or hide them under the bucket.
Spacing time with a daily note was a logical thought—although somewhat confused! I was, however, somewhat confused. Basing time on body rhythms was erroneous.
The human circadian cycle varies, from 22 hours to plus 24 hours (24 hours 40 minutes is the length of the Martian day. I don't know why I settled on that).
I propose to review what has happened as honestly and accurately as possible. I shall use as many pages as is necessary.
This pad is a hundred pages thick and I don't suppose They will keep me here forever.
First fact: I was assaulted, choked unconscious.

I came to, briefly, in a vehicle. I think it may have been a van—I had the impression of space, and more noise than is normal in a car.

When I moved, someone swore, and struck me twice in the face with a closed fist. Once in the left eye, once on the mouth. The blows stunned but didn't particularly hurt me. Somebody put a boot heavily on the back of my neck, and then a sack was forced over my head. The sack smelt earthy—perhaps a potato sack?

Fact 2: there are at least 3 people involved.

I was carried bodily out of the vehicle by that number. I was laid on a hard surface and all my clothing and possessions were removed. Watch, glasses, suit.

Stripped. I was still half-stunned and could not resist.

The sack was put over my head again. I saw nothing but blurred light while it was off, and the close weave prevented seeing anything when it was on. The strippers, who may also have been the carriers, made no sounds.

I was again carried, I presume to the door of this room.

I heard the door opened. I was stood up, held by at least two people (2 sets of hands to either arm).
Another person planted a boot against the small of my back, and must have caught hold of the sack at the same time.
They pushed hard: the sack was dragged off my head as I was hurled onto the floor. The door slammed shut. When I was able, I wound the towel around me, and wrote the first page.
I do not think I was functioning normally for some time.
Fact 3: the room.
I estimate it to be 12 feet long and eight feet wide.
The ceiling is at least ten foot tall. I know that, averagely, the head is one 7.5th of the length of the body, and that the extended arm is, averagely, 3 head lengths. Say, 26 inches. I am five foot seven and one half inches tall. The light is fixed to the ceiling. A white plastic shade protrudes around it. Arm outstretched, it is, I estimate, 2 feet beyond my fingertips.

Thursday, 4

The light has never been turned off.
Even if I stood on top of the excrement bucket, I could not reach the bulb to remove it.
The bucket would not support my weight.

The walls are made from wood, pine planks?
They reach from floor to ceiling. They are varnished, clean, and very solid. I tried hitting them. There was no hollow sound, indicative of thinness.
The floor is covered with grey linoleum. There is no baseboard.
The door appears solid. There is no handle or visible lock on my side.
I think this room is soundproofed. Listening intently, all I can hear is the rushing of my own blood, that sealike hiss in the ears.
Designed to hold prisoners? Speculative nonsense.
Fact 4: myself the prisoner, the hostage, the kidnap victim.
But why? Who on earth would want to kidnap a university lecturer of English?

Thursday evening

There is a routine!
The door opened two minutes ago. The hooded man with his iron bar came in and said,
'Don't say a word.'
He put down another apple, another rigger of water.
'Tomorrow morning, put the bucket by the door.'
As he backed out, he said,
'Sweet dreams, man.'
The sarcasm apart, I feel elated.
Lightheadedness from lack of food? (I have had one apple in at least two days. Enough water, however.)
I do feel definitely better being oriented in time.
I have walked back and forwards until I feel tired.
I began doing this this morning, partly to get warm and partly to get rid of a persistent cramp. I had not realised how hard a floor is, when slept upon.
Nor how much one needs coverings. I am very cold.
What was the secret of the Indians of Tierra del Fuego?

Friday morning

Woken by something banged against the door.
A voice called,
'Stay by the wall.'
When the door opened, the man with the crowbar stood to one side, and another smaller, more slender person entered.
I feel certain it was a woman although I couldn't ascertain breasts. Hooded also. She put down a full rigger of water, and removed the bucket and the empty water container. The door closed after them.
There was a blank cream wall opposite the door.
Two things bother me: for one thing, there is absolutely no sense in kidnapping me. I have no special knowledge (unless one is vitally interested in post-modernism). I can hardly postulate a rival in the department.
Secondly: why leave me with writing materials?
To keep my mind off the situation? Skewed thinking, surely.
I can think of—unlikely reasons. For instance, let me come to rely on this talking to paper and then break me, by removing the pen and paper. Why?
It makes no sense.

Friday afternoon

I have decided to divide each day into 3.
I recall reading—Arthur Koestler?—that they best survive captivity who keep mentally busy and physically fit.
So, after the bucket exchange in the morning, I shall pay meticulous attention to personal hygiene.
I shall then write a morning page.
I shall then walk. The room is 12 feet long. Five easy paces. Ten room lengths is 40 yards; 44 x 10 will be a mile. I shall walk 2 miles and then rest.
It is a pity I don't know any isometric exercises.
After resting, I shall write an afternoon page, a reminiscence, recalling pleasant times in the past.
Today: seafood extravaganza. A wok of golden oil. A smiling hostess-cook, kimono-clad, skin smooth and golden. It is Hawaii, not Japan, and the air is scented and warm. By the wok, a wooden platter of small fat purplish prawns, readyshelled. Slit in half by the practised knife of the smiling cook (a mysterious smile, soft, hinting).
Dipped in thin riceflour batter, quickfried in the boiling oil.
Dip, hiss, spatter, and out onto the cooling rack.
Goldly crisp without and softsweet white succulency within.

Friday night

This has been a good day.
I feel positive and oriented.
I walked three miles in the afternoon.
I resolutely ignored the craving for food, particularly fat, that I seem to have developed, by thinking of the benefits of this style of living—three days on water and apples, with much more exercise than I am accustomed to, must rid me of fat, must be preventive of coronary occlusions. One can live for many weeks, fasting, providing one has a sufficient liquid intake. I have enough water.
My captors inflict inconvenience and discomfort but they must intend my survival.
The nightly apple arrived some time ago. I started to ask 'Why am I' and was halted by a wave of the iron bar.
To be hit with that thing . . . ! I shrugged, with dignity.
I savoured the apple.
(Reading back over these notes, I recognise a silly oversight. Nowhere have I put who I am! Harrod Wittie, doctor of philosophy, bachelor gay, late of Cranford Court, now residing in Limbo . . .)
My mother gave me my name, and I have grown fond of it. It was a childhood crucifixion—Horrid, How Odd, Herald, Hard Rod etcetera—but now it is a distinction. No common Harry, I.
There is a scrabbling sound along this back wall. A mouse.

?Saturday ?Morning

No bucket transfer/collection/exchange.
I must have been concussed. It has just occurred to me that Baghead could easily lie, tell me goodnight while it was the middle of the day.
I feel very depressed, and tired beyond all reason.

I have just remembered that the prawns in Hawaii, that lovely night of amber flesh and tempura, were supposed to be still alive until the moment of slitting.
'For sweetness' smiled the Japanese lady cook.
Unshelled, unshelled, and every raw exposed nerve quivering with pain.

Sometime later, before night
(if it's night when they bring the apple)
(if they are going to bring an apple)

My vulnerability. I am not particularly strong.
My pectoral muscles hang fatly. I work—no, I loiter, lilybound in the ivory tower, sucking bee-flowers. Garnering others' honey. Mulcting the hive. A true academic, a scholar with soft white hands.
Protection. One slightly soiled towel. It smells.
There is a strong ammoniac reek everywhere, even though the bucket is still lidded.
Weapons. Rigger filled with water. Club?
Stab with the felt-tip pen? Throttle with the towel? Kick? Bite? Gouge?
I am not a fighting man, My father used to call me 'Nancypants', which was cruelly unfair. (Also, 'You four-eyed slob', which was descriptive albeit unkind.) I have never liked hurting anything, and fighting involves hurting.
Plan of attack. Throw the unmentionable contents of the bucket? Hurl a water-club at the Baghead?
Stab at his face with pen. Wait until woman Baghead comes, grab her as hostage. Ridiculous.
I am sitting against the wall unmoving except my hands. It is warmer if I don't move. This spot grows quickly cold. The scrabbling noise is back. Gnaw away, little mouse. Freedom is the other side of the wall.

Sunday?

There was no apple, but somebody must have stolen in and
emptied the bucket while I slept.
I have walked about a mile.
When I woke, I was so stiff and cramped that I groaned,
literally groaned, on sitting up.
The walking has taken away most of the stiffness, but the hip
I slept on, the side-buttock muscles—gluteal?
still feel sore. There is a dull bruise-like patch there.

Day continued, before apple-time

I have been thinking, unwillingly, of all the people who are, or were, close or dear to me. My mother. My aunt Bethel. My father. Randall Hayhurst. Jaban.
Jaban with the little golden dragon hung around her dark neck and the winkle of diamond in her earlobe.
My mother lived with her sister, Bethel. She went there when my father left for the war. When he came home, he immediately left for a wild area in Southland, where he hoped to break in land for a farm. My mother waited for suitable quarters to be built there for her, and died, waiting.
I don't remember her well, because she died when I was 4. I always associate a particular food with her (softboiled eggs mixed in with squares of buttered white bread, all the crusts trimmed off—it sounds sickly, but is nourishing reassuring food). When she died, my father tried to look after me for one dreadful year. I don't remember any of it, just my aunt's words: 'You came back full of asthma and bruises.'
The farm must've been breaking my father in, by then.
I never returned to him while my aunt lived. She died when I was 14.

Randall Hayhurst was the English master at the district high school I was obliged to go to, after I had come to live with my father. He was a tall aloof tattered man who only took notice of me after I had my glasses broken outside his classroom.
'You are a big lad, Wittie. Are you a big boob?' I turned violently red and said I was a pacifist, and would not demean myself striking a fellow human. He smiled thinly. 'You are also a big fool. See me after this class.'
I was afraid of being caned. Instead, he was gentle, even tender towards me, lending me a book by Bertrand Russell, giving me a note for my father saying my glasses had been broken at sports. One thing led to another, led eventually to university, led to this career and—one could see such a paradigm of ridiculous cause and effect and end—led to this room.
He had a favourite phrase, 'Boy, this is a rite of passage.' 'Boy, consider these as rites of passage.'
Randall Hayhurst died while I was an undergraduate.

The apple at last. More water. Not a word. Just the threat of an iron rod. I swore at the closing door. There was a sound like a chuckle, as it closed.
A dark kind of chuckle, just as the voice has a supple, a moccasin rhythm.
I am upset. I do not swear. It is a slovenly looseness of mind and tongue. That much of my father's teaching I respect. The only time I heard him swear was a New Year's night 20 years or so ago. He was drunk-sick on port and kept hiccupping. Indrawn hiccups, ready to throw-up. His RSA cronies had long left. I was 22, newly M.A., reluctantly keeping him sneering company into the New Year. He said.
You know nothing. Degrees hah. Hiccup. You'd know nothing. What about Sidi Rizeg?
(That's what it sounded like.)
The kind of drunken question one cannot answer except maybe with What about Sidi Rizeg. I kept silent.
He mumbled then, staring into his glass, Two mon-months later went back and there were these panzer men die Panzer Mensch dried already like old mum-mummies lips sealed back from their protruding teeth and one with a wrist rubbed to the ivory bone above his wristwatch rubbed to ivory bone by the wind sanding the skin away.

My father the thief

He rubbed his own wrist.
He belched.
I smelt port and bile.
He said,
Wrist bone . . . knobby bits . . . took the fuckin' watch tho.
He must have torn it away, minute rags of dried flesh still adhering to the back.
Brown skin.
My father spat.
Life would make a fuckin' dog sick, he said.
He drank himself comatose that night.
When he died, when the land finally claimed his sick eroded body, when his shrivelled heart finally burst, I looked everywhere for the watch from Sidi Rizeg.
I found his medals, with carefully-printed obscenities inked on the ribbons.
I could not find the watch.

I am very tired.

I have slept.
For the first time since this started, I recall dreaming.
I keep a dream diary at home.
How many nights I have lost!
I am standing in a long shadowed gallery. Someone says out of the dark, 'The children are burning, be aware!'
I look down and see a dead head, clearly dead because it was tautskinned, browned, mummified. As I look, a thousand tiny rays of light beam out as though minute holes or the very pores of the skin are emitting light. Like a strange jackolantern and not terrible at all.
A gentle voice says
'As well as being initiation into mysteries, as well as being social demarcations, they are to be considered times of getting to know yourself, learning intimately your capacity for pain, your outer limits of endurance.'
There is a smell of chalkdust.
The head smiles at me and the teeth grow longer, the lips paler and thicker. It bleats at me. It is a sheepshead.

I woke shaking.
I have been thinking deeply about this dream.
I feel—not quite present.
I feel very ill.
I cannot stop shaking.

[TUESDAY MORNING]

Someone has written
TUESDAY—MORNING
on this page.
The little heap of pages has been straightened tidily.
I have a new towel.
The bucket has been emptied.
There is a strong smell of Jeyes fluid.
I must have fainted.

Tuesday evening

The Baghead has brought not only water, not only an apple, but a BOWL OF HOT SOUP!!!
A kind of chicken soup I think.
He stood by the doorway, nodding at me occasionally, thumping one end of the iron bar in his hand. He is no longer wearing gloves—or maybe I never noticed before.
His hands are dark brown and look enormous.
At the end of the soup I said thankyou.
He nodded, gestured for me to pass back the bowl.
Daringly I asked, Why am I here?
He shook his head, he chuckled. It was a deep pleasant chuckle. He closed the door carefully.
I felt like crying.
The soup in my starved belly feels so good.
I must pull myself together.
I must think SURVIVAL.
Whatever this ordeal is, I can endure it, I must survive it.
It must have meaning, however pointless it seems. I will survive until the morning.

The scrabbling noise has returned.
Welcome back, mouse!

Tuesday evening 2

Thinking about that dream:

There was a smokedried head in the Dunedin Museum. We saw it on a school trip to the city. The custodian pointed out the shallow dent at the back where the deathblow had been dealt. He also pointed out minute holes in the left temple; the work, he said, of a kind of borer.

Anthropology 1, and a lecture about Egyptian mummies. Believed by that people to be the permanent home of the spirit, the ka, (or was it the ba? That would explain the bleating). If destroyed, the ka had no home, no viability. How many mummies were destroyed by grave robbers searching their cerements for amulets and jewels. How, by evidence of charred remains, it was deduced that, at one interment in Thebes, the mummies of children had been set alight to provide grave robbers with torches.

Tuesday evening 3

I feel quite cheerful contemplating these gruesomenesses.
The effect of food.
Also, it may be imagination, but the room feels warmer, as though some kind of underfloor heating has been switched on. The kindness of kidnappers . . .

Did you know that, even until the beginning of this century, groundup mummies were a principal ingredient in some bituminous paints?
The tarry sides of aunt Bethel's woodshed. Built before the first world war, tarred to keep the seawind from eating away the boards. Load of old wogs wearing away in the wind . . .
As to what the dream meant—

The mouse appears to have stopped. A pity.
Other prisoners adopt rats and cockroaches.
I should like to follow historical precedent.

Wednesday, change of bucket

My dream continues to haunt and provoke me.
It definitely contains a message. If I can unearth it.

I have always hated sheep. I presume this hate dates from my father's abortive attempt to rear me.
I cannot think of their pale knobby faces, narrow skulls, blank silver eyes with that oblique slit of pupil, without feeling sick. Their shitbesmeared backsides, fat protruding anuses.
Yet we live by courtesy of the gushing blood, the raw carcasses, the woollen skins of sheep.
My father praised sheep. A sheepfarmer was the noblest of professions. To be a shepherd was a high calling.
A man, his crook, his maud, his dogs—a man and his flock of sheep—that's how our world began, our civilization started, he said.
And we keep the world going today, he said.
Dead sheep: naturally I've seen many. From my father butchering a cull for dog-tucker (and our breakfast chops) to the flayed bloody line adangle at the works.

Wednesday, change of bucket 2

I remember coming to a mudhole and seeing, I thought, a nearly dead sheep, still feebly struggling.
The river ran by the edge of the mudhole.
I hate seeing things hurt, so I went to aid the sheep.
Plunged to nearly kneelevel in the mud. Knew by the stench the thing was dead. It was the river toying the head, making it jiggle, making it look alive.
I lost one of my gumboots in the mud.
In a last ironic gesture, the rotting neck gave way (or did an eel seize it? Tug it off) while I hunted for my boot.
The head swirled slowly round, bared teeth grinning at me.
Then it went downstream to freedom and the sea.
What this means is—incomprehensible.

Wednesday, appletime.

I have been walking again, not the frenzied pace of days before; a gentle meditative strolling, restful to body and mind.
I have eaten my apple.
I am starving for fat.
I thought the belly shrunk with fasting?
There are new folds in my chest, and flab where before was stiff paunch. But my hunger has not abated.
Think of thick roundel of pork, brown crisp crackling, and then the tender cream almost waterylooking fat, and next to it the pinklybrown rich roast meat.
Or, a fat smoked pickled chicken, the preserved meat like the finest prosciutto ham.
Or, thin slice of smoked raw ham encasing a ripe fig-half, the roll topped with a blob of piquantly flavoured whipped sour cream.
It does not help.
That bloody mouse is gnawing again.
I locate where it is by crawling along the base of the wall and listening carefully. I find the place. It is marked by a large knot in the wood, about an inch from the floor.
I kick there, hard.
The noise has stopped.

Thursday, bucketchange

Water. I am sick of water.
I have never been drunk in my life but if someone passed in a large jug of of even moonshine I'd gladly gulp it all down right now.
I know. Carbohydrate need. The demanding body.
Against it, think: alcohol: poison. Each swallow wears off another layer of tongue and palate cells, shreds the stomach-lining, buggers more pancreas and scars more liver fatty liver, burns a little more brain. 'Neat drink, eh?' Gulp it down Jack, it's a splendid way to go if you don't mind fenestrations and a drooling mind that forgets what happened a minute ago.
Still, still, I would give a lot for a good meaty drink—

there was a clink just then.
The centre of the knothole I kicked last night just fell onto the floor.
Nothing else.
I must admit to being disappointed at no quivering pink nose, no beady black eyes.
I've looked in the little hole. Darkness. Poked the felt-tip in and waggled it around. Space all around.
Still, a hole leading out . . .
I've put the bit of knothole carefully back.
No sense in letting even a semifriendly Baghead know.

WE WERE KIDDING
TODAY IS TUESDAY
MORNING

bad bad bad time
think
SURVIVE
Think of survivors who were victims too.
Jews survived Dachau. Some of Daddy Sharpe's followers survived his aborted uprising. We heard of slaves who escaped the ovens.
Then the one pipi in the sack, the sack we had collected at the beach and carelessly forgot about and the pipis yawned died in the sun, but that one pipi stayed resolutely closed. And how aunt Bethel laughed when I asked we take it back to the beach. All that way! she said. It's crying for cool sand, I said. Show me tears, she scoffed. And the shellfish on my hand bled out a little of that infinitely valuable salt ichor it had hoarded. And despite that, my aunt dug it in with its brothers, garden manure.
Hate. Think hate. Jew for Nazi. Slave for Jamaican planter. Anonymous meals for their devourers here in gentle God-zone.
I could grow my fingernails to knifelength naturally sharp claws eye-threats watchit!
How long o my god how long?
I am beaten before I start. Heroes wouldn't feel like this. Heroes would spy out the weakness of the foe.
What is the weakness of an iron bar? The weakness of a big hooded black man? The weakness of a dark laughing voice that doesn't hear questions, doesn't hear pleas?

Two can play games.
Very well.
The only day I am certain of
was Tuesday. Very well.
This shall be Tuesday.
Tuesday 28. I shall not
count either of Their notes.
I used one to wipe myself before.
I have a kind of diarrhoea.
The water tastes of plastic.
My towel is beginning to stink.
Emissions.
My hair has tangled to hard lumps
in places, and when I rubbed my
mouth before there was some pale dried
deposit in my growing beard.
I am not in good physical shape.
I don't care.

XXXI
the illiterate black morons

Fact 1 = kidnapped for unknown reasons
by unknown people
Fact 2 = unknown black people
Fact 3 = the only black I've ever known
in all senses of the word
is Jaban.
She has strange friends. The one
who told me how to kill people with
a length of vanadium steel wire.
The laconic one with blurred eyes
and dirty rustyblack locks corkscrewing
out of his skull. Stink of marijuana.
She, the linguistics expert, chatting
nonsense with other blurred people.
'Til Jah came, til I came I.'
'We all in Babylon not of Babylon.'
'Ras Tafari seized I out.'
Jaban smiling.
Come taste my wet pink lips she says
whose lips are purplish and fat.

What did I say to Jaban by the fire?
What did I say when she lost her earring?

3XII
The one of the vanadium steel wire

Leaving a thumbprint on a pulse
thinking of
a wand of wood
poked into an eye

thinking of
a yard of silk scarf
and the thinness of necks
how brittle we are!

thinking of
poetic combinations
brass jackets and charcoal
lead and saltpetre
a little native Sulphur

thinking of
stroking you
over the nerve clusters
make and break death and joy points
leaving a thumbprint
on that pulse

I have spent hours thinking this. I have
never succumbed to poetry before. The
vanadium wire expert told me the easy
way to kill yourself. Quick jab to the
vagus nerve and you step forever
outside yourself
a found scholar, a poet manqué

XXXIII, bucket time

This is absurd.
The Baghead said, ‘You alright man?
Want to call it off? Want to say the word?’
And when I asked what word, call *what*
off, he hit me over the shoulder with the bar.
There is a pink and grey bulging welt
there. No bones broken.
Japanese monks in zazen woken with
bamboo blows.
What word?
Call what off?
Am I insane?
Is this a harsh equivalent of a padded cell?
I have just reread everything and I make
sense to myself. My writing looked under
stress at the beginning but flows now.
The water tastes more of plastic.
What word?

I have recounted and to my shame
it is XXX2

We had been talking of rites of passage.
Jaban said there were none in our society.
Driver's licence, I said. 21st parties.
She claimed them faded examples, futile,
no virtue because no mystery and no pain.
She was lying in my arms. It was an evening of perfect calm.
The driftwood fire had burned down to shadows and embers.
She lay in my arms, frowning at the fire, her hair a black
aureole, springy, warm, exciting. What would you make us as
rite of passage? I asked it as a joke.
Design it yourself. She became grumpy.
She frowned more at the fire. Firewalking?
I put my lips against her velvet skin.
She said, On some Pacific Islands, the dead relations of an
abortion collect it and raise it to shadowy adulthood in the
realm of the dead. Such creatures at maturity, I joked again,
darting in and out of the portals, the swinging gates,
the bar-room doors between here and hereafter!
The sturdy hero breed, larger than life. Our Mauitikitiki
fishing for islands with his grandma's jawbone
and sneering at the overheated sun.
No son, she said.
In the silence after, the sea sounded too loud.
She lay in my arms, little, compact, black,
and I lay by the fire, content on the edge of
mystery. Become a man for me she whispers.
Rites of passage make strange beasts I said
and laughed and she wrenched away.

The button of wood in the wall fell out.
There was a timorous scrabbling noise.
I smiled, waiting for the mouse.
The futility of it all.
Two FINGERS came through.
Little and dirty.
And brown.

This is XXXIII. My fingers cramped
yesterday with that thready writing.
They are still sore and seem swollen.
I have fingers on the brain!

3IV, appletime

Isn't it strange?
The fingers are back. There was a startled silence, like gladness, when I touched them. They withdrew quickly, came back, feeling round the edge of the knothole. I folded a piece of paper and gave it to them. The paper rustled through the wall. I put my eye to the knothole, could see nothing but darkness—the entrance hole must be at an oblique angle, big enough for a child to get its hand?arm into its side of the wall. The fingers have just come through again, poking out a crust of bread. It is grey and stale, but it is bread.
I whisper at the knothole, Who are you?
Where are you? Do you know who I am?
There is silence only. I cannot even hear breathing.

3IV, appletime continued

I have just been thinking, with
calmness and gratitude, of the
patience of that child, whoever
it is. Working away at—what?—
a loose board?
Why?
Is it also confined?
Is this a place of prisoners?
At least it is fed better.
I did little drawings on the last two
sheets of paper. Another crust.

3V

Suppose it isn't a child at all?
There are very small coloured people.
Jaban stood only 4 feet 11 inches.
Suppose They all sit in there and
watch their thing feed rubbishy
scraps through my precious hole,
smothering giggles?
I pass through another sheet of
papers, soon as the fingers appear.
I get a button.
Mouse I whisper, dear Mouse, give me food.
There is silence. The fingers have gone.
I put the knothole back.

My urine in the clean bucket looks thick and cloudy and orange. I am ill? Urinoscopy is a dead art.
There is a sore the size of a fifty cent coin on my hip, and I stink.
I keep shutting my eyes and yawning. O I don't know why.
I am tired of trying to get answers. Dragging answers out of stones. I am not slow enough, longlived enough to dance in the tenth dimension, to understand its ponderous crystalline speech.
I have said, Rites of Passage. I have said, Jaban.
I have been hit twice. My shoulders ache.
This is pointless.

Tuesday appletime

I read back to where I am cold and I
quake with mirth. It is so hot here now.
Underfloor heating definitely, redhot wires
through the concrete floor, and it all cooking
me. I shall wind up dehydrated, mummified,
and they will be able to stash me away in a
ceiling-space with no fear of rot-smell
giving the corpse's game away.
The fingers come out the hole, and wait.
Dear Mouse, here is paper for you

Tuesday

Who will come looking for me?
Who will even know I'm gone?
Jaban has gone back to Nui Niu
Gineau Ginea, Randall and Bethel
and Mother and Father all mould.
Hello Mouse. Have another sheet.
I am halfway through this pad.

O THE PAD
THE PAD
When it is used up this sentence
of weird imprisonment will cease.
I shall feed all the sheets through
the wall. Silent Mouse shall lessen
my onerous days. Cheating? Ah the
cunning of the hand defeats the mind!

I have stuffed 18 sheets into the
hole.
No more will fit.

Tuesday bucket time

I heard the paper being withdrawn.
The usual space of silence.
Then the paper *came back*
Horrifying. I am stunned.
We had established our barter system
Mouse and I. Paper, then food, or
button or something. Not return/
When the fingers came through again,
confidently open, brown, I crushed them against
the wall hard as I could. Barefooted yes
but I ground my foot down. I didn't hear
much noise.
Horrifying. I hate hurting. What am I?
What am I? What am I?

I cannot find the knot in the wall
I cannot find where the hole was
I cannot find

Time span
(it is Tuesday)
even the days lost their names the gods their days
A paper a day but I have given them away
squirrelling in the wall by small
brown mice probably torn to bits
O MY GOD ALL MY DAYS
there is Jaban's antiseptic voice
velvet voice no *antiseptic humour*
Litter? Shitpaper do you think? What else
does the writing of this world come
to
no how else does the writing

to grow up means
to be alone
to grow up
means to be
alone
to grow up
you must know you have reached
manhood and you are now grown
up
I feel five years old
and far in the madding

—breaking down a proud ship's sail mulching it with the
underpants of a black whore to make the bright paper
for this raggy boke
tar and sedimental dirt and elemental juices ghostly
amongst the print
what pleasures she knew! and pains
What winds it gathered, harnessed, proudly ploughing Ocean!
What ruinous dispersion into fibres, flax or hemp or
cotton or maybe silk of an insect's mummy cocoon turned
grave drawn apart to this strange papyrus end

No
this is just trees with their vital juices squashed out
an acid cocktail, residue

I am very clearheaded and very weak
i am harrod wittie doctor of philosophy
failed lover failed test failure man

nobody has come into the room for days

there is no water left

my flat I give to whoever wants it
my books to the university senior common room

a thinning grey layer between me and vegetativeness

I do not understand

i would like to take the door of the
neck so nobody shall take my body's
pitch but i think it will too weak

this is absurd this is absurd
it is absurd
this is absurd

i am not crying

goodbye Jaban my mother
goodbye dad you bastard
goodbye kind Randall of the fingers
give the pipi to Beth a bethel is
a seamans church
goodbye mouse